JU_ BOOTS

JENNY NIMMO

Illustrated by
PAUL WARREN

HEINEMANN · LONDON

William Heinemann Ltd
Michelin House
81 Fulham Road
London SW3 6RB

LONDON   MELBOURNE   AUCKLAND

First published in 1990
Text © Jenny Nimmo 1990
Illustrations © Paul Warren 1990
ISBN 0 434 93076 8

Printed in Italy
by Olivotto

A school pack of BANANA BOOKS 37-42 is
available from Heinemann Educational Books
ISBN 0 435 00106 X

Chapter 1

'WRITE ABOUT YOURSELVES!' Miss Cosmo said, and everyone got out their pens and roared away over their pages, telling about their hair and their eyes and their wonderful pets, their mums and dads and radio-controlled toys. Some people are so lucky.

I wrote, 'My name is Timothy and my feet hurt!'

'What's that supposed to mean, Timothy Starr?' Miss Cosmo said, looking over my shoulder.

'It means my feet hurt!' I replied, 'and you smell of baby powder, Miss!'

'Oh, do I? Just carry on with the writing, Timothy,' she said, and then she sighed. It was hard to tell if her sadness was for me or for herself.

'Have you got a bush-baby, Miss Cosmo?' I asked.

'If you're trying to ridicule me, Timothy, you're failing miserably,' she snapped. 'Look, no one's laughing. No one's even smiling. So just get on with your work.'

She drifted away taking her baby smell with her. Poor Miss Cosmo; she can't afford to powder herself with lilac or honeysuckle rose. She has to use the cheap baby brand. There are three babies in my home so I'd know that smell anywhere. Her mum's an invalid, I'm told, and that's expensive! But it wasn't impossible that Miss Cosmo *could* have a bush-baby. I saw letters from Australia stuffed into the top of her bag while she was waiting for the bus.

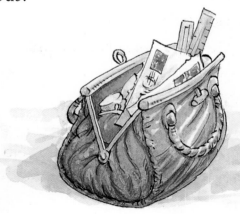

Miss Cosmo always smiles at Leo; his work must be wonderful; a ray of light in her bleak and disappointing day. Leo's an only child so he does all right; music lessons, Spanish holidays, two pairs of shoes, all that kind of stuff. He's still my mate though. I go to his place sometimes. In the kitchen his mum listens to operatic arias while his dad cooks chilli con carne. They've put hi-fi equipment on shelves where the baked beans ought to be, and a

fluffy brown spaniel sleeps on the sofa.
I wish I had a dog! They keep
books in the lavatory. I learnt that
Jupiter was King of the Gods sitting on
Leo's toilet, in fact I reckon I've learned
almost everything I know in there.

To the sentence I had already written
I added, 'There are three babies at
home. One's been there for three
months, it's called Anna and it screams
at night. One crawls and it's got a daft
name because my mum's husband is

foreign. He isn't my dad. The eldest isn't really a baby. Aurora's nearly three and she walks; Aurora Borealis I call her, it's a name for the wonderful lights that glow in the Northern sky sometimes, though Aurora isn't much like a wonderful light, she's mousy and miserable most of the time.

Miss Cosmo wasn't interested in my efforts. She told us we'd have to finish our work tomorrow. It was time for fresh air.

Chapter 2

THE OTHER BOYS went out to practise
football. I couldn't hardly kick the ball,
my feet hurt that much. So I sat and
watched. My toes were all twisted
inside my shoes and there were blisters
on my heels so I couldn't run. There
was a hole in one sole and the weather
got in and squeezed my toes with icy
fingers. I told Mum my shoes didn't fit
but she just sighed and said, 'Oh,
Timothy, you can't mean it, they're
almost new. The baby needs a winter
coat, Alessandra's gone through all her
tights and Aurora's got to have a bed.

Where's the money coming from I'd like to know. My Gino's not a millionaire.'

Almost new! That was a joke. They were bought when we went to Southend for August Bank Holiday. That was at least six months ago. If Runaway Harry, my father, were here would he have taken me to buy some shoes, I wondered. I like Gino a lot but he works all day and half the night, even on a Sunday. I didn't want to bother him. He had other problems.

After school I always walk home with Leo. We go down Wildoak Road, then he turns left into a tree-lined square of pastel houses. I cross the road and hobble down Carmody Street to the flats.

When my feet were really bad I'd look in Heale and Hyde, the shoe shop

on the corner. Well, I could dream,
couldn't I, about wearing flashy
trainers or real shiny leather? For a few
seconds my toes would dream with me.
They'd be walking on fur or feathers. I
could almost feel them smiling. 'O.K.'
I'd tell them. 'I'll give you a treat
tonight. I'll nip in the bath before
Mum's pulled the plug after the girls.'
The water was always cold when it
came to my turn.

On that particular afternoon there was a sale on at Heale and Hyde. The shop was packed, and outside people shifted about and squeezed in to get a better look at the bargains. I didn't need to go any closer. I could see the Jupiter boots from the road. They were high on the peak of a glittery cardboard mountain. They were orange and gold and a great red hurricane stormed across each toe in a fiery flash. There were sixteen silver moons encircling the midnight cuffs and streaks of blue and white thundered up each side. I had 60p in my pocket, left over from crisps. 'Everything Half-Price,' said the sign in the window. I went in.

It was stuffy in that shop and it smelled of tired feet. I stood near the window. The assistants hopped about under shelves, up ladders, down on

their knees, faces red, fingers fumbling. What a job! 'Is it for you or your little boy?' one said to a woman beside me. The woman looked at me and then away as though I didn't exist. She pointed to a pair of red spiky things on a table.

Linda from next door was lolloping around behind an armful of boxes. I could tell it was Linda because she's nearly six foot tall and her hair's the colour of foxgloves.

I turned my back on them all and stared at the Jupiter boots. There was a ladder near the window. I climbed up and stretched out. The ladder wobbled a bit but no one seemed to notice. I begged my fingers to grow so that I could reach the boots and they did. It was the beginning of Jupiter's magic!

First one boot and then the other; I had them under my arm. I came down the ladder and stood there for a whole five minutes. No one came. No one asked me if I wanted to try on or pay. My sad feet cried out for those boots. 'I'll borrow them,' I thought, 'just to give my toes a treat for an hour, then I'll bring them back.' I put the boots in my school-bag and walked out, through the crowd of frantic ladies all trying to be Cinderella.

Chapter 3

IN THE DARK behind 'The Happy Friar' fish and chip shop, I took off my hated achy shoes and dropped them on the ground. I pulled the Jupiter boots over my scraggy socks, up and up, over my jeans, up to the knee. Of course they fitted. There had never been any doubt about that. But the warmth of them spread further than my knees; it travelled out to my fingers, swam round my neck and sang in my head.

And then something happened that amazed and frightened me. Fire flickered in my boots. Hot colours swirled over my feet and crawled round my legs. It was like watching flames caught in a bottle. The Jupiter boots were glowing in the dark. I closed my eyes because it was all so scary. And when I did that, ice-cold air rushed over me and the ground slid away. I was flying! Higher and higher and higher. I hugged myself to keep from falling. No one will believe this but I flew past the moon, I know I did. I couldn't have dreamed the frost that tingled over my scalp. I couldn't have invented the rumbling of a thousand unknown volcanoes, or the strange smells of alien atmospheres. It was all too scary. 'Can we go now,' I said to the boots. 'I'm not quite ready for

this!' And they took me down, gentle
as anything. I didn't open my eyes
until I felt the ground safe beneath me.
And there I was, lying between the fish
and chip bins again. I felt quite shakey
as I set off back to Heale and Hyde.

But the shoe shop was closed. All
dark. I rang the bell. No answer.
'Please!' I cried. 'I've brought your
boots back!' A tiny window, very high
up, glimmered for a second, but it
didn't open. Frost began to glitter on

the pavement. It was so cold. I had to go home wearing the boots because I'd left my shoes behind in the dark.

'Where've you been, Starr?' Mum always flung my runaway dad's name at me when she was worried.

'Got held up,' I said.

'You know I get worried when you're late.' She stared at my feet. 'What have you got on?' she said.

'Boots!'

'I can see that! Where did you get them?'

'Leo!' I said.

'Oh yes? His mum's chucking out her finery is she? They're ladies' boots, Tim. Take them off?'

'I haven't any others.' I told her. 'I dumped them.'

'You what?' Little red warning lights appeared on her cheeks. The baby in her arms began to cry. 'What is it, darling?' She snuggled baby Anna up to her angry cheek. Alessandra tried to crawl into her lap. 'What, you too?' She sighed and coughed her smoky cough. She could look so pretty if she tried. She's got lovely blue eyes and real curls, has my mum, but she looks so tired these days.

'I want a drink!' Aurora said. She always wants something when Mum has an armful of babies.

'Can't you wait?' Mum sighed.

Aurora began to snivel.

Mum looked round for a place to put two babies, but both began to cry.

Aurora didn't like that. She stood and roared. Her whole little body shook with rage, and all at once I knew it was just as bad for her as it was for me, worse perhaps, because she was

there all day, in the mess and the
smoke and the crying.

'Come on,' I said and I grabbed her
sticky fingers.

'Where are you going? Aurora's got
no coat?' Mum cried.

'Trip to Outer Space!' I informed
her. And we were gone.

Chapter 4

OUTSIDE I HEAVED Aurora onto my shoulders and piggy-backed her fast down five flights of concrete steps. She sobbed great shuddering sobs all the way down.

Complaints poured out of doors and windows. 'What's Timothy Starr doing now?' 'Leave that kid alone!' 'He's up to no good again, just like his father!'

'Mind your own business!' I told all those nosy so-and-sos.

We ran down to the shabby square of grass where tiers of lights surrounded our impossible launch-pad.

'They're closing in, Aurora,' I shouted. 'We'll have to hurry. Get ready for take-off. Close your eyes,' I ordered. 'Now hold tight, tighter than you've ever held anything in your whole life! We're getting out of this, Aurora! Count, Aurora, ten, nine, eight, seven, six, five, four, three, two, one . . . Blast off!'

She couldn't count backwards and she was still snivelling but she managed a choked little 'Blast off!'

It worked. We levitated; left them all behind. All the crying babies and grumbling grown-ups. We smoothed out of the world and into the glittery sky, and Aurora's tears were swept away, sparkling crystals, icy in the outer atmosphere.

We passed the cold empty moon and sailed on to the stars, until we found him, blazing beside us; the giant rolling in colours. His wild-fire storms showered us with gold and we glowed.

'Look, Aurora!' I cried. 'It's Jupiter, King of the Galaxy. He gave us happy flying boots so we could be warm forever.'

Aurora chuckled into my neck and Jupiter sang to us; crooned in our ears like an affectionate father, murmured deep sympathy and musical understanding.

Aurora chanted 'Ring 'o Roses'. I joined her with one of Leo's kitchen arias, and we all sang together.

'Let go now, Aurora, you won't fall,' I said. 'I want you to fly all by yourself!'

Aurora's brave, I'll give her that,

because all those millions of miles
away, she set herself adrift in space,
and there we were, the two of us,
touching fingers just in case, and
Jupiter gave my flying sister's shabby
dress a great spring clean; covered her
with stardust, green and pink and gold.

'You're shining, Aurora!' I said.
'You *are* the Northern Lights. I'll bet
they can see you for miles!'

She wasn't mousy any more; she
was a planetary princess!

I sang and sang until I had no breath

left. My throat began to burn and I
realized that great Jupiter, for all his
thoughtfulness, could hardly avoid
turning us to crisps if we lingered
beside him for too long. And so,
because I wanted us to enjoy another
visit, I decided we'd better go home
before we ended up as blazing
satellites.

Down we went! But I missed the
runway; the Jupiter boots slipped on a
bottle and our landing was a shambles.
Aurora lay on her back and laughed,
and so did I.

The local teenagers were there, yattering at the bottom of the steps. They looked at us giggling on the grass and Linda from next door said, 'You're barmy, Timothy Starr!'

'And you're a pink hedgehog,' I said.

Aurora jumped up and we marched past the teenagers, very proud. They'd never get to where we'd been.

Chapter 5

GINO WAS THERE when we got back. Life with Gino is never dull. He and Mum are either throwing plates or kissing one another. He has a funny accent and his English is all back to front, but he's stayed with Mum for four years now, and that's more than Runaway Harry ever did.

'What you got there, Teemee?' he asked, looking at my Jupiter boots.

'Great aren't they?' I said. 'My mate gave them to me!'

'Very fine!' Gino said. 'Real cowboy stuff!'

'You've got it wrong, Gino,' I explained. 'They're Jupiter boots!'

I forgot to get in the babies' bath that night but I didn't need to. My feet were really happy. I didn't have to spend hours comforting them. I nodded off as soon as I'd tucked my Jupiter boots safe under the bed.

Chapter 6

NEXT DAY WAS Saturday. I knew I had to go back to Heale and Hyde but I couldn't resist strutting in the Jupiter boots, just one more time. I was King of the Comfy Feet. I didn't care about the teasing. Teenagers don't scare me.

'Look at 'im!'

'Who do you think you are, Timothy Starr?'

'Thinks he's the Queen, doesn't he?'

And the threats; 'Dropped off a lorry did they, Timothy Starr?'

'They'll nab you, just like they did your dad!'

'Watch it, Timothy Starr!'

'You'll soon be smiling the other side of your face!'

I didn't care. My happy feet carried me about, warm and proud. I meant to take the boots back, I really did. But I was too late!

A white car crawled through the cold afternoon. It stopped outside our flats. Two people in black uniforms got out; a man and a woman. I was prancing on the steps. The woman asked me to take them to my mum. I lead the way. I wasn't frightened or ashamed, just sad. 'Goodbye, Jupiter boots!' I said.

I took the police into our flat; past the piles of washing and into our

living-room where Mum was ironing.
Gino was being a horse for two babies.
No one was crying, not then.

'Good afternoon!' Sergeant Clarke
coughed to clear a way for the bomb he
was about to drop.

Mum went as red as boiled beetroot,
though she wasn't the guilty one.

Sergeant Clarke and WPC Potter
introduced themselves. 'We've come
about your son. Items are missing from
a certain shoe shop!'

Everyone stared at the Jupiter boots.

Mum went very still and held so tight to the ironing board, I thought she was going to fall. Then Gino got up and, very carefully, put Anna into her arms. 'It's a mistake!' he said. 'Teemee doesn't steal. Teemee's a good boy!'

So Sergeant Clarke told them about Heale and Hyde and the boots that were going cheap. They hadn't been missed until they closed the shop. Then someone saw me, recognized the boots, and knew they hadn't been paid for. I reckoned it was Linda from next door, but I never did find out.

'Oh, Timmy,' Mum suddenly cried.

'Why did you do it, son?' asked WPC Potter.

'My feet hurt,' I said.

They were foreign words to them. No one seemed to understand. It wasn't the answer they wanted, but it was the only one I had.

Gino crouched down and pulled off my boots, very gently, and then my socks, one by one, and everyone saw my horrible feet.

'Poor Timmy!' Aurora shook her head.

'Good grief!' exclaimed the WPC, 'the poor lad's had his feet stuffed into shoes two sizes too small, I'd say!'

'With chilblains 'an all,' added the Sergeant.

In winter the afternoon sun smiles right into our window, and all our shabby furniture is spellbound into being almost beautiful. When my mum knelt beside Gino, the sunshine sparkled in her hair and there were tiny drops of gold shining in the corners of her eyes.

'I'm sorry, Timmy,' she said. 'So sorry! Forgive me!'

'You're my mum,' I told her. 'And I would have paid. I don't want to nick things, do I? I don't want to be like Runaway Harry. I want to pay for things, but where's the money? I'd clean the car if we had one. I'd deliver the papers if I had a bike, I'd do anything for some cash!'

They didn't speak. Mum fumbled with Anna's bald head and Gino scratched his curly one until he had an idea. 'Look, I pay for the boots, yes? Then everything's all right!'

The Sergeant said he didn't know about that but if Gino went round right away and paid, perhaps Heale and Hyde would forgive me. However, I'd better keep out of trouble in future.

'This is a very serious matter!' Sergeant Clarke said as he laid a hand on my shoulder. It was a heavy hand and it made me think of judges, prison and bread and water.

Chapter 7

WE WENT ROUND to Heale and Hyde there and then, Gino and I and the police. Mr Hyde said he knew the boots were in a sale but he hadn't meant to *give* them away. He was happy with the money Gino offered. 'Lucky for you, I'm in a good mood,' he told me. He was a funny little man, like a dwarf made out of leather; his face was full of wrinkled smiles, the sort of person who would answer questions, I thought, so I pushed my luck and asked, 'Where did the boots come from, Mr Hyde?'

He darted me a look under his scraggy eyebrows and I knew that he understood. 'It's a funny thing,' he said, 'but we've no idea. They just arrived, as it were, in a silver box; no name, no number, not even a size.

They could have come . . .' he stopped in mid-sentence, leaned very close to me and whispered, 'from Outer Space!'

'They did!' I whispered back.

Sergeant Clarke and the WPC were beginning to look uncomfortable. They saw that justice had been done and left the scene of my crime, but not without a warning. 'If there's a next time,' said the Sergeant, 'you'll be in real trouble, Timothy Starr! Understand?'

I nodded. I knew there wouldn't be a next time.

'And now,' said Gino, 'we want trainers, very smart, so Teemee can keep his special boots for . . .'

'. . . night rides?' Mr Hyde's bright little teeth gleamed in a smile that threatened to split his face in half. Then he departed, through a velvet curtain; no going down on knees for him.

So hedgehog Linda had to fit me up with new shoes. Gino insisted on the best. They were washing-powder white with starry pads on the toes, long laces and thick springy soles.

Linda put my Jupiter boots in their proper silver box, and Gino didn't give her rude remarks a chance. 'You're a lovely girl, Linda,' he said and turned her scowl into a smile.

'Thanks, Gino! You're the greatest,' I told him. 'And I'm sorry for all the trouble.'

'I know, Teemee,' Gino hugged me like a real dad. 'Gino's your friend, he'll get you what you need. But don't take things no more, or it's the end of happiness for all of us!'

'I won't let you down, Gino,' I said, 'never. But I want to pay you for the boots. I want to earn some money!'

'Why don't you take Aurora out for a bit after school. Give your mama a break! 25p every day!' he said.

'Brilliant!' I cried. We'd go behind the flats, where teenagers couldn't spy on us. And we'd shoot off to Jupiter. Aurora would like that. We'd explore every star; there are so many we could be happy for the rest of our lives.

Mum looked anxious when she saw my new shoes. 'Where'd you get the money, Gino?' she asked.

'Darling Maria,' he said. 'Tips! Gino's a good waiter, very polite, knows all about wine. Everybody loves him. You must trust your Gino, he's not like Runaway Harry!' and the crazy Italian swept my mum off her feet and into a wild waltz. And all the babies laughed instead of crying, and I pushed my luck just once more and asked, 'Can I have a dog, Mum?'

'Don't be daft, Timmy, we're five floors up, remember?' my spinning mother sang.

No, Timothy! No dogs, that's too much to hope for! No pets, only Jupiter boots, paid for now, warm and bright, to keep always and forever, so that you can travel out whenever you want, far away.

Next Monday, Leo couldn't take his eyes off my new trainers. 'Brilliant!' he said. 'Wait till my dad sees them. He's just got to get me some, too.'

I was happy to get back to my writing. I wrote about my Jupiter boots and how they'd taken Aurora and me on a journey we'd never forget. I told how they'd made my feet smile and how the sun had beamed into our home and turned mum's tears to gold.

'You're a bit of a poet, Timothy,'

Miss Cosmo remarked, scanning my pages with a smile.

'It's not a poem,' I said, 'it's the truth!'

'All the way to the stars?' she said.

'All the way,' I said. 'Just think, Miss Cosmo. If boots can carry me to Outer Space, what could the right pair of shoes do for you? Australia's not so far away, when you think about it?'

She didn't walk away this time, she stared through the window at chilly winter clouds and said, 'Perhaps you're right, Timothy. Perhaps you're right!'